George MacDonald's

THE CARASOYN

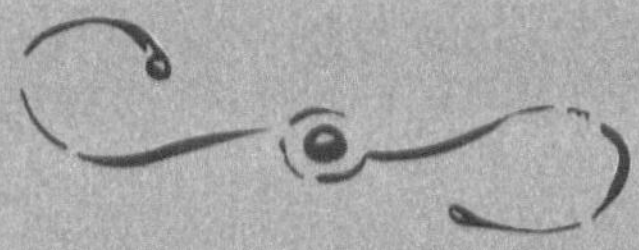

ADAPTED BY:
JEROME TILLER

ILLUSTRATED BY:
MARC JOHNSON-PENCOOK

Adapted Classics for Middle School
An imprint of ArtWrite Productions
1555 Gardena Ave NE
Minneapolis, MN 55432-5848

Book Design by ArtWrite Productions
Edited by John Leitner
Cover Design by Kristina Brown

ISBN 978-1-939846-26-6

adaptedclassics.com

kristinadesignz.com

artwriteproductions.com

PREFACE

The *Adapted Classics* Collection

Contemporary-classic illustrations in *Adapted Classics* books add expression to visually-rich stories by world-famous authors. Lightly modified and illustrated to suit and attract modern young readers, stories in the *Adapted Classics* collection are respectful renditions of timeless stories from the world of classic literature.

View the entire collection at: www.adaptedclassics.com

Dedicated to the Campbell Clan:
Dave, Mary, Chris, Claire, Aaron & Gene

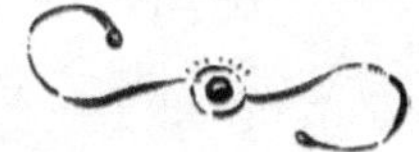

Once upon a time in a valley in Scotland, there lived a boy about twelve years of age. He was the son of a shepherd and had no sister or brother. When his father was out all day on the hills with his sheep, the boy was all alone, as he had been forever, for his mother had died the day he was born. Yet, when his father came home every night from the hills, he was always sure he'd find the cottage neat and clean, the floor swept, a bright fire, and his supper waiting for him, just as if there was a wife willing to look after his household instead of only a boy.

Fact is, although Colin was a full-time homemaker and could only read and write and had no knowledge of figures, he was ten times wiser and more capable of learning anything than if he had been at school all his days. Hard knocks here and there were teaching him well, and he was never at a loss when anything had to be done. Somehow he could always blunder onto the straight road to his end while others were still putting on their shoes to go look for it. And yet, all the time that he was busiest working, he was also busy building castles in the air, just as if the two separate pursuits ought always to go together.

And even though Colin was industrious, he was never overworked; he had plenty of time to himself because he made sure it would be that way. In winter he spent his time reading by the fireside or carving pieces of wood with his pocket knife. In summer he always went out for a ramble. He took great delight in a little stream that ran down the valley from the mountains above.

He would wander up this run of stream every afternoon with his hands in his pockets, getting so absorbed in watching the stream's antics that he almost never got very far upstream. Sometimes he would sit on a rock staring at the water as it scolded, protested, and muttered while hurrying through the stones, always having its own way. Sometimes he would stop by a deep pool and watch the crimson-spotted trouts darting about as if their thoughts, not their tails, sent them where they wanted to go. And when he stopped at the little cascade, tumbling smooth and shining over a hollowed rock, well, he seldom got beyond that entrancing sight.

But there was one thing that always troubled him. When the stream came near the cottage, it could find no other way to go than through the little yard where the cow-house and the pigsty stood. There, not finding a suitable channel, it spread abroad, becoming more like a puddle than a brook. And it was made all muddy there with the treading feet of the cow and the pigs, and defiled some too with their droppings.

In fact, the stream looked quite lost and ruined near their cottage. It slipped away out of the yard as if ashamed, with poverty-stricken speed, its forces spent. The stream took a long time to gather itself together again. At length though, receiving the friendly help of a brook coming straight from the hills, it gathered heart and bounded on afresh.

"The stream gets so weak when it passes through the yard. The cow drinks some, but that's not making much of a difference," said Colin to himself. "Bossy isn't dirty, or doesn't mean to be— but she is stupid and inconsiderate. She'll drop pies anywhere without a thought. The pigs don't drink from the stream, but they are the dirtiest slobs possible. It wouldn't surprise me a bit if the stream takes offense at being dashed about by their trampling and wallowing around. Something must be done."

He surveyed the whole ground to find a way to reroute the stream. But the lay of the land offered only one feasible solution; the only other course the stream could take besides its current one lay right through the cottage.

To most engineers this would be a non-starter, but Colin's heart danced at the thought of having his dear brook running full strength right through the house. How cool it would be in the summer! How convenient for cooking and how handy at meals! And then the music of it! It would tell him stories and sing him to sleep at night! What a companion it would be when his father was away! And then he could bathe in it when he liked. In winter—nah! But winter was a long way off. Don't need to be spoiling a good plan by thinking about winter!

The very next day his father went to the fair, so Colin set to work at once. It was not such a very difficult undertaking.

The walls of the cottage, and the floor as well, were hard clay. The sun had dried the walls nearly into a brick, and the floor had been trampled hard. Both, however, could still be worked with pick-axe and spade. He cut through the walls, and dug a channel along the floor, laying in stones on the bottom and sides. After the stream got out of the cottage and through the small garden in front, he figured it should find its own way to the channel below, for here the hill was very steep. He had accomplished a lot in a short period of time because he was strong for a boy, and firmly committed as well.

That evening his father came home."What in the hallowed halls of Edinburgh have you done, Colin?" he asked, in great surprise when he saw the trench in the floor.

"Wait a minute, father," said Colin, "till I get your supper, and then I'll tell you."

So when his father was seated at the table, Colin darted out. He hurried up to the stream and broke open the bank right in the place where a natural hollow led straight to the cottage. The stream dashed out like a wild creature from a cage and shot through the wall of the cottage.

His father gave a shout, and when Colin went in, he found him sitting, holding his spoon half-way to his mouth, his eyes fixed on the stinky, muddy water that rushed foaming through his floor.

"It will soon be clean, father," said Colin, "and then it will be so nice!"

"But it isn't clean looking or smelling right now, and I'm eating! Geez, Colin. You've got a lot of nerve!"

Colin began listing the many advantages having a brook running through their house would bring. At length his father couldn't help but smile. "You are a curious creature, Colin. But why shouldn't you have your fancies as well as older people? We'll try it awhile and then we'll see about it. And by the way, you were right. I notice the stink has almost disappeared."

The fact was, Colin's father had often thought what a lonely life the boy lived. And it seemed hard to take from him any pleasure he could find. So out rushed Colin, hopeful to see if the brook would indeed take the shortest way headlong down the hill to its old channel. It did, and to see it go tumbling down that hill was a sight worth living for.

"It is a mercy to all living creatures," said Colin, "that the stream has nobody's bones to break, or it would break twenty in a minute. It flings itself from rock to rock right down the hill, advancing with abandon just as I would like to do if it weren't for my bones."

All that evening he was out and in without a moment's rest, now up to the beginning of the cut, now following the stream down to the cottage, then through the cottage, and out again from the front door to see it dart across the garden and dash itself down the hill.

At length his father told him he must go to bed. He took one more peep at the water which was running quite clear now, and obeyed. A short while later, his tired father also shut down his day and retired to bed to sleep the night away.

THE FAIRY FLEET

Colin's bed was about a couple of yards from the edge of the brook, and since he always got up first in the morning, he slept at the front of the bed. So he lay for some time gazing at the faint glimmer of the water in the dull red light from the sod-covered fire while listening to its sweet music till its murmur changed into a lullaby and sung him into his deep sleep.

But soon he began slowly coming awake again. The busy stream had added loud, strange sounds since he dropped into dreamland—the noise of boards knocking together, but also a tiny chattering and sweet laughter. He opened his eyes. The moon was shining along the brook, lighting its surface, but only an occasional glimmer escaped betwixt the crowded boats of—what in the jings—a fairy fleet?!

Colin slapped his face until he was convinced he was awake. The sailors on the boats were as busy as sailors could be, mooring along the banks or running their boats high and dry on the shore. Some manned little sails which glimmered white in the moonshine—the sails were either half-lowered or blowing out in the light breeze that crept down the course of the stream. There was activity everywhere—tiny voices calling, tiny feet running, tiny hands tugging at ropes that ran through blocks of shining ivory.

On the shore stood groups of fairy ladies in all colors of the rainbow—green predominating. They were waited on by gentlemen all in green with red and yellow feathers in their caps.

The queen had landed on the side of the stream next to Colin, and all at once twenty paired dancers were swinging along the shores of the fairy river. And there lay Colin's great-big face, just above his bed-clothes, glowering at them like an ogre.

At last, after a few dances, he heard a clear sweet, ringing voice say, "I've had enough of this. I'm tired of doing klutzy dance moves like clumsy big people. Let's have a game of Hey Cockolorum Jig!"

That instant every pair sprang apart, and every fairy began frolicking alone. They scattered all over the cottage, and Colin lost sight of most of them.

While he lay watching the antics of two near him, who behaved more like clowns at a fair than the gentlemen they had been a little while before, he heard a voice close to his ear. He looked everywhere about his pillow, but he could see nothing. The voice stopped the moment he began to look, but began again as soon as he gave it up.

"You can't see me," said the voice. I'm talking to you through a hole in the head of your bed. And don't look for me. If the queen sees me, I'm pinched. Don't rat me out!"

The voice, maybe a little panicky, sounded as if its owner was of high rank, so Colin followed the order.

"Please, listen up. I am a little girl, not a fairy. The queen stole me the minute I was born, seven years ago, and I haven't been able to get away. I suppose you don't believe in fairies. I wouldn't either, I guess, but what the heck—it is what it is. I was only a new-born when they captured me, so I get to wondering sometimes whether I believe in humans. You know what I mean?"

Colin rattled his head from side to side and filled his cheeks with air, trying to clear his mind.

"But anyway, I don't like the fairies. What they did, stealing me away! They are so, so evil. And totally dafty! They never grow any wiser. Hey, I grow wiser every year—like you maybe. That's the main thing that makes me so different than them."

Colin stuck his fingers in his ears, held his breath, and grunted as hard as he could. But no change of scene.

"I want to get back to my own people, but they won't let me. They make me play at being somebody else all night long, and I sleep all day. That's what they do themselves. And I should so much like to be myself—like you, except, of course, I'm a girl. The queen says being myself is not the way to be happy at all, but I do want very much to be a little girl. She robbed me of that! Do take me."

"Wow! I have to be sleeping! I gotta wake up. This is interesting, but it's too real"

"Get a grip—you are not sleeping. Don't you get it? We're doing this live, right now, and we gotta move fast. Are you with me or not?"

How am I to get you?" asked Colin in a whisper, which sounded as sweet as the wind in the willows compared to the soft but coarse voice of the female whatever.

"The queen is pleased to purple-flush all over with you. It's that brook thing you did. She is sure to offer you something in return for doing that. And that means me! Make that demand and stick to it. You savvy? Now do it! Here she comes."

Immediately he heard another voice, shriller and louder, in front of him. Looking about, he saw standing on the edge of the bed a lovely little creature wearing a crown glittering with deep violet jewels and holding a reed for a scepter in her hand, the purple blossom of it shining like a bunch of garnets.

"Oh, you big, bug-eyed creature! What are you staring at? Face to face with a fairy, are you? Ha! I don't know how ya see with them bug eyes! They're much too big and letting in way too much light. Be ready now, you tube! I'm gonna fix that."

So saying, she laid her wand across Colin's eyes. In that instant, he saw the room like it was a huge barn, full of creatures about two feet high. The beams overhead were crowded with fairies, playing all kinds of tricks, scrambling everywhere, knocking over each other, throwing dust and soot in each other's faces, peeping and grinning from behind corners, dropping on each other's necks, and tripping up on each other's heels. Two had got hold of an empty egg-shell and, coming from behind one who was sitting on the edge of the table and laughing at some other fairy on the floor, they tumbled the shell over his whole, entire self so that he was lost in the cavernous hollow.

In stark contrast to these rough shenanigans, the lady-fairies mingled and bothered with none of these childish pranks.

Their tricks were always graceful, and they had more to say than things to do. They lent a faint air of dignity to the scene.

After the queen had suited herself in giving Colin these strange sights by laying her wand across his eyes, she put herself into a serious pose, for she had some formal things she wanted to say.

"Know, son of a human mortal, that thou hast pleased a queen of the fairies. Lady as I am over the elements, I still cannot have everything I desire. One thing thou hast given me. Years have I longed for a path down this stream to the ocean below. Your horrid farmyard, ever since your great-grandfather built this cottage, was the one obstacle. For we fairies hate dirt, not only in houses, but in fields and woods as well, and above all in running streams. But I can't talk this way any longer—I'll cut it short and tell you what it is. You are a dear good boy, and you shall have exactly what you please. Ask me for anything you like. Go ahead—anything is yours"

"May it please your majesty," said Colin, very deliberately, "I want a little girl that you carried away some seven years ago the moment she was born. May it please your majesty, that's what I want. I want her."

"Not! No way! It does not please my majesty," cried the queen, whose face had been growing very cross. "That's my girl—I raised her. Ask for something else."

"Then, whether it pleases your majesty or not," said Colin bravely, "I hold your majesty to your word. I want that little girl, and I will have that little girl and nothing else."

"You dare to talk to me that way, you thick!"

"Yes, your majesty."

"Then you shall not have her."

"Then I'll turn the brook right back through the dunghill," said Colin. "You think I'll let you come into my cottage to play these fairy hijinks as you please, especially if you treat me like this?"

Colin sat up in bed and looked the queen smack in the face. As he did so, he caught sight of the loveliest wee creature peeping round the corner at the foot of the bed. And he knew she was the little girl because she looked pretty, bold, and sassy, fitting perfectly with the voice he had heard. Yet she also emitted an aura that was mysteriously subdued, oddly combining all those traits while also sucking her thumb.

The queen, up against Colin's stubbornly firm resistance and perfectly aware that queens in Fairyland are absolutely bound by their word, began to try another plan with him. She put on her sweetest manner and looks, and as she did so, the little face at the foot of the bed grew troubled. Immediately, the head which hosted the little face shook from side to side so vigorously that her thumb popped out of her mouth.

"Dear Colin," said the queen, charm oozing, "you shall have the girl. But you must do something for me first."

The little girl shook her head even faster while giving Colin the eyeball, but to no avail—for he was bedazzled by the charm of the queen and dead-focused on her.

"To be sure I will. What is it?" he meekly said.

And with that response, he completely blew the deal. He was now bound by a new bargain, and totally in the queen's power.

"You must fetch me a bottle of Carasoyn," said she.

"What is that?" asked Colin.

"A kind of wine that makes people happy. Like port, but way more effective. Some incredibly powerful stuff."

"Why? Are you not happy already?"

"No, Colin," sighed the queen. "Not happy enough."

"You have everything you want."

"Except the Carasoyn," returned the queen.

"You do whatever you like and go wherever you please."

"That's just it. I want something out there, something to do that I have not yet already liked, something to take me elsewhere, someplace I know not where, but a place that I darn well please to go. I want some very special something that I know nothing about. I want a bottle of Carasoyn."

"You don't know anything about it? I thought you said it was a happy wine, like port. Whatever that is."

"I've only heard about it. That's it—I've just heard about it." And at this she cried like a spoiled child, not like a sorrowful woman.

"But how am I to get it for you?"

"I don't know. But aren't you the same smart fella that did the brook thing? So then go figure it out."

"Wait! That's not fair," cried Colin. "You said I could have anything I wanted. Are you backing out on me? But you can't! You gave me the fairies word! You're honor bound!"

The queen burst into a fit of laughter, and bounding away to the side of the river, jumped on board of her boat. Like a swarm of bees, the courtiers and sailors gathered from every which direction of her boat, two creeping out of the bellows, three out of a basket-hilt on the wall; six out of the flour-tub, all powdered white.

Then more rushed from all parts of the cottage to the riverside. Amongst them all, Colin spied the little girl creeping aboard the queen's boat. She shot Colin a withering glance of scorn before she adjusted her pinafore to cover her eyes while the queen shook her fist at her. Within five minutes all had scrambled either into the queen's boat or support boats, and just like that, the whole fleet was in motion down the stream. In another moment the cottage was empty, and everything had returned to its usual size.

"They'll be all dashed to pieces on the rocks," cried Colin, jumping up and running into the garden. When he reached the cascading falls, there was nothing to be seen but the swift plunge and rush of the broken water in the moonlight. He thought he heard cries and shouts coming up from below, and fancied he could distinguish the sobs of the little maiden whom he had so foolishly lost by bargaining with the queen.

But the sounds he heard might be only those of the water. He couldn't tell, for to all the different voices of a running stream, there is no end. He followed its course all the way to its old channel but saw nothing to indicate any disaster.

He crept back to his bed, where he lay thinking what a fool he had been to fold his winning hand. He was a loser. The queen, using fairy magic to neutralize him, made him powerless by luring him into a new agreement. Now he could do nothing except meet the terms of her new demand for Carasoyn, whatever that was. He lay awake berating himself and crying over the bold and sassy little girl who now would never become a woman. He eventually drifted off to sleep imagining just how complete a woman she would've made!

THE OLD WOMAN AND HER HEN

In the morning, however, his courage had returned, for the word Carasoyn was repeatedly saying itself in his brain.

"People in fairy stories," he said to himself, "always find what they want. Why shouldn't I find this Carasoyn? It doesn't seem likely that I will, but the world doesn't go 'round by likely. I'll try."

But how was he to begin? For an answer to this he reasoned at length until he could stand no more.

"Why go on so," he finally said aloud. "If the Carasoyn grew in the fairies' country, the queen would know how to get it. So what am I doing wasting my time puzzling over fairyland?"

Just at that moment and all at once, he remembered the time he had lost himself on the moor when he was a little boy and that hut he had found with an old woman inside. She was spinning wool, but before long, she was taking him on the strangest head trip ever ! She told him such fantastic stories before showing him the way to get home. He thought maybe she could help him out, for even though she was ancient and wise back then, she'd be even older and wiser now—provided she's still alive and spinning. It couldn't hurt to give it a try!

So he left the stream and climbed the hill, and soon he came upon a desolate moor. The sun was clouded over and the wind was cold, and everything looked quite dreary. There was no sign of a hut anywhere, so he wandered on looking for it until he realized he had forgotten his way back. At that exact instant he knew he was lost, and seeing the hut he was looking for right before his eyes, remembered it happening the same way back when he lost himself that first time!

"It seems the way to find some things is to lose yourself," he mused.

He went up to the cottage, which was like a large beehive built of turf, and knocked at the door.

"Come in, Colin," said a voice. So he entered, stooping low to get through the little door.

The old woman sat by a fire, spinning away at an old-fashioned wheel with a distaff and spindle. She stopped spinning the moment he entered.

"Come and sit down by the fire," she said, "and tell me what you want."

Then Colin saw that she had no eyes.

"I am very sorry you are blind. You weren't when I met you as a little boy." he said.

"Never you mind that, my dear. I see more than you do for all my blindness. Tell me what you want, and I shall see what I can do for you."

"How do you know I want anything," asked Colin

"Now that's what I don't like," said the old woman "Why do you waste words? Words should not be wasted any more than crumbs."

"I beg your pardon," returned Colin. "I will tell you all about it."

And so he told her the whole story.

"Oh those children!" said the old woman. "They are always doing some mischief. They never know how to enjoy themselves without hurting somebody. I really must give that queen a bit of my mind. Anyway, my dear, I like you. I will tell you what must be done. You shall carry a bottle of Carasoyn to the silly queen. She won't like it! I could've told her that. But that's my business. First off, you must dream three days without sleeping a wink. Next, you must work three days without dreaming a bit. And last, you must work and dream three days together."

"Excuse me—how am I to do all that? Are you kidding me!"

"Don't disrespect! I will help you all I can, but a great deal will depend on yourself. In the meantime you must have something to eat. You're a scrawny lad, I can see that", she said, making would-be eye winks to send a clear message.

Then she rose and, going to a corner behind her bed, returned with a large golden-colored egg in her hand. She laid it on the hearth and covered it over with hot ashes and started chatting away to Colin about his father, and the sheep, and the cow, and the housework, showing him that she knew all about him. At length she drew the ashes off the egg, and put it on the plate.

"There—eat that chookie-poo. It'll put some meat on your skinny bones."

"It shines like silver," said Colin."Which is pretty amazing, but not all that appetizing."

"Silver signals that it's done." The old woman set a knife and fork before Colin. "Eat it."

Despite the way it looked to him, Colin had never tasted anything half so nice. And he had never seen such a quantity of meat in an egg. It was a hearty meal.

"Shall I tell you a story while you have your dinner?"

"Oh, yes, go right ahead," answered Colin. "You told me such great stories before! You've got a real knack for it."

"Thank you. I will then. But first—hey Jenny," said the old woman, "my wool is all done. Get me some more."

And from behind the bed came a plain-colored, but large and beautifully-shaped hen. She walked sedately across the floor, putting her feet down daintily, like the prim matron she was. Stopping by the door, she clucked.

"Oh, the door is shut, is it?" said the old woman.

"Let me open it," Colin managed to say while swallowing the forkful of egg and meat he had just shoveled into his mouth.

"Do, my dear."

"What are all those white things?" he asked, looking out of the open door and across the land, for the cottage stood in the middle of a great bed of grass with white tops.

"Those are *my* sheep," said the old woman. "You will see."

Into the grass Jenny walked, and stretching up her neck, gathered the white woolly stuff in her beak. When she had as much as she could hold, she came back and dropped it on the floor, picked the seeds out and swallowed them, then went back for more.

The old woman took the wool, and fastening it on her distaff, began to spin, giving the spindle a twirl and then dropping it and drawing out the thread from the distaff. But as soon as the spindle began to twirl, it began to sparkle all the colors of the rainbow. And the hands of the woman were no longer old and wrinkled as they drew out the wool; they were young, long-fingered and fair.

The spindle spun and flashed, and the hen kept going out and in, bringing wool and swallowing the seeds, and the old woman kept telling Colin one story after another. He thought he could sit there all his life and listen to them.

Sometimes it seemed that the spindle was flashing the stories, sometimes that the long fingers were spinning them, and sometimes it seemed the hen was gathering them off the fields of the long dry grass and bringing them in her beak and laying them down on the floor.

All at once the spindle grew slower and gradually ceased turning; the fingers stopped drawing out the thread, the hen retreated behind the bed, and the voice of the blind woman was silent.

"I suppose it is time for me to go, " said Colin.

"Yes, it is," answered his hostess.

"Please tell me then, how I am to dream three days without sleeping?"

"That's over," said the old woman. "You've just finished that part. I told you I would help you all I could."

"Have I been here three days, then?" asked Colin in complete astonishment.

"And nights too. So Jenny and I and the spindle are quite tired now and want to sleep. Besides, Jenny is holding back three eggs she needs to lay. Make haste, my boy."

"Please, then, tell me what to do next."

"Jenny will put you on the right way. When you get where you are going, tell them the old woman with the spindle desires them to lift Cumberbone Crag a yard higher and to send a flue under Stonestarvit Moss. Jenny, show Colin the way."

Jenny appeared and, muffling clucks under her breath, led him a good way across the heath by a path this hen only could have found. Then, still mumbling, she turned suddenly and walked home, leaving Colin to wonder again just where he was.

THE GOBLIN BLACKSMITH

Colin could just perceive something suggestive of a track, which he followed till the sun went down. Then he saw a dim light before him. Keeping his eye upon the light, he came at last to a blacksmith shop where, looking in at the open door, he saw a huge, hump-backed blacksmith working with a sledgehammer in each hand. He was a strong, awful looking creature, with sharp, pointed teeth and a red ball for a nose

The blacksmith grinned out of the middle of his breast when he saw Colin, and said, "Come in, come in. My youngsters are lonely. They will be glad of you."

The moment Colin entered, the blacksmith took a huge bar of iron from the furnace and began laying his two sledgehammers on it so that he disappeared in a cloud of sparks, and Colin had to shut his eyes and be glad to escape with a few burns on his face and hands. When the iron had been beaten till it was nearly black, the smith put it in the fire again, and called out a hundred odd names:

"Here Gob, Shag, Latchit, Licker, Freestone, Greywhackit, Mousetrap, Potatoe-pot, Blob, Blotch, Blunker—"

Whatever word he spoke, or when his words were interrupted by a laugh or sneeze, he did not stop working one moment. As often as the sparks flew in his face, he snapped at them with his eyes (which were the color of a half-dead coal). Now with this eye, now with that one, the more the sparks got into his eyes, the brighter they grew.

And as he called, one dwarf after another came tumbling out of the chimney in the corner in which the fire was roaring. They crowded around Colin and began to make hideous faces and spit fire at him. But he boldly faced them and stood his ground. At length one dwarf pinched him. Colin could not stand for that, so he struck him hard on the head. The strike rang the dwarf's head like an iron pot and gave Colin such a jar he thought he had busted his own hand to pieces.

"Come, come, young man," cried the blacksmith; "you keep your hands off my children."

"You gotta tell them to keep their hands off me then," said Colin.

Just as the dwarfs began to crowd about him again with even more spiteful looks, he recalled the message the old woman had given him to pass along.

"Stand back, you imps! I won't take abuse from you any longer. I got work for you to do—and directly. Now listen up. The old woman with the spindle says you are to lift Cumberbone Crag a yard higher and send a flue under Stonestarvit Moss. And she don't mean maybe either, little folks! She's dead serious."

In a moment they had vanished in the chimney. In one moment more the blacksmith shop shook to its foundations. But the blacksmith took no notice. He only worked more furiously than ever. Then came a great crack and a shock that threw Colin on the floor. The blacksmith reeled, but never lost hold of his hammers or missed a blow on the anvil.

"Those boys will do themselves a mischief," he said. Then turning to Colin, "Here, you sir, take that little hammer. This is no safe place for idle people. If you don't work you'll be knocked to pieces in no time."

The same moment there came a wind from the chimney that blew all the fire into the middle of the shop. The blacksmith dashed up upon the forge, and rushed out of sight. Presently he returned with one of the goblins kicking and screaming under his arm. He held him by the neck, laid his ugly head down on the anvil, and hit him a great blow with his sledgehammer right above the ear. The hammer rebounded, the goblin gave a shriek, and the blacksmith flung him into the chimney, saying:"That's the only way to serve him. You'll be more careful for a little bit of a while, I guess, won't you Slobberkin?"

And thereupon he took up his other sledgehammer and began to work again, saying to Colin: "Now, young man, as long as you get a blow with your hammer in for every one of mine, you'll be quite safe. But if you stop, or lose the beat, I won't be answerable to the old woman with the spindle for the consequences."

Colin took up the hammer and did his best. But he soon found that he had never known what it was to work. The blacksmith worked a sledgehammer in each hand, and it was all Colin could do to work his little hammer with both his hands, which made it a terrible exertion to go blow for blow with the blacksmith.

Once, when Colin lost the time, the blacksmith's sledge-hammer came down on the head of his little hammer, beat it flat on the anvil, and flung the handle to the other end of the shop, where it struck the wall like the report of a cannon.

"I told you," said the blacksmith. "Now here's another hammer. Make haste, for the boys will be in want of you and me too before they get Cumberbone Crag half a foot higher."

Presently the biggest-headed of the goblin family came in out of the chimney.

"Six-foot wedges, and a three-yard crowbar!" he said, "or Cumberbone will soon cumber our goblin bones."

The blacksmith rushed behind the bellows, brought out a bar of iron three inches thick or so, cut off three yards, put the end in the fire, blew with might and main, and brought it out as white as paper. He and Colin then laid hammers upon it till the end was flattened to an edge, which the blacksmith turned up a little to put the crow in the bar. He then handed the tool to the imp.

"Here, Gob," he said, "run with it, and the wedges will be ready by the time you come back."

Then to the wedges they set. And Colin worked like three. He never knew how he could work before. Not a moment's pause, except when the blacksmith was at the forge for another glowing mass!

And yet, to Colin's amazement, the more he worked the stronger he seemed to grow. He was developing his own set of pipes! And

instead of being worn out, the moment he had caught his breath he wanted to be at it again; he felt as if he had grown twice his size since he took the hammer in his hands.

And the goblins kept running in and out all the time, now for one thing, now for another. Colin thought if they made use of all the tools they fetched, they must be working very hard. And the convulsions he felt in the shop proved that; they were well hard at it somewhere out there in the neighborhood for sure!

And the longer Colin worked together with him in the shop, the more friendly grew the blacksmith. At length he spoke, each and every word adding energy to his blows.

"What does the old woman want to improve Stonestarvit Moss for?"

"I didn't know she did want to improve it," returned Colin.

"Why, anybody may see that. First, she wants Cumberbone Crag a yard higher—just enough to send the north-east blast over the Moss without touching it. Then she wants a hot flue passed under it. Plain as a sledgehammer! What did you ask her to do for you? She's always doing things for people and making my bones ache."

"You don't seem to mind it much though, sir," said Colin.

"No more I do," answered the blacksmith as he delivered a blow that drove the anvil half way into the earth, from which it took him some trouble to drag it out again. "But I want to know what she is after now."

So Colin told him all he knew about it, which was merely his own story.

"I see, I see,"said the blacksmith. "It's all moonshine; but we must do as she says notwithstanding. And now it is my turn to give you a lift, for you have worked well. As soon as you leave the shop, go straight to Stonestarvit Moss. Get on the highest part of it, make a circle three yards across, and dig a trench round it. I will give you a spade. At the end of the first day you will see a vine break the earth. By the end of the second, it will be creeping all over the circle. And by the end of the third day, the grapes will be ripe. Squeeze them one by one into a bottle—I will give you a bottle—till it is full. Cork it up tight, and by the time the queen comes for it, it will be Carasoyn."

"Oh, thank you, thank you," cried Colin. "When am I to go?"

"As soon as the boys have lifted Cumberbone Crag and bored the flue under the Moss. It is of no use till then."

"Well, I'll go on with my work," said Colin, and struck away at the anvil.

In a minute or two the same goblin whose noggin his father had hammered came in and said, respectfully, "It's all right, sir. The boys are gathering their tools and will be home to supper directly."
"Are you sure you have lifted the Crag a yard?" said the blacksmith."Quite sure?"
"Slumkin says it's a half-inch over the yard. Grungle says it's three-quarters. But that won't matter—will it?"

"No. I dare say not. But it is much better to be accurate. Is the flue done?"

"Yes, we managed that partly in lifting the crag."

"Very well. How's your napper?"

"It rings a little."

"Let it ring you a lesson, then, Slobberkin—for the future."

"Yes, sir."

"Now, master, you may go when you like," said the blacksmith to Colin. "We've nothing here you can eat, I am sorry to say."

"Oh, I don't mind that. I'm not very hungry. But the old woman with the spindle said I was to work three days without dreaming."

"Well, you haven't been dreaming, have you?"

And the blacksmith looked quite furious as he put the question to Colin, lifting his sledgehammer as if he would serve it to his napper as he had to Slobberkin.

"No, I haven't," answered Colin. "You took good care of that."

The blacksmith actually smiled.

"Then go along," he said. "It is all right."

"But I've only worked—"

"Three whole days and nights," interrupted the blacksmith. "Get along with you. The boys will bother you to death if you don't. Here's your spade and here's your bottle. Now get!"

THE MOSS VINEYARD

Colin did not need a bigger hint than that—he was out of the shop in a moment. He turned, however, to ask the way; there was nothing in sight but a great heap of peats which had been dug out of the moss standing there to dry. Could he be on Stonestarvit Moss already? No help.

The sun was just setting. He would look out for the highest point at once. So he kept climbing, and at last reached a spot from where he could see all round him for a long way. Surely that must be Cumberbone Crag looking down on him! And there at his feet lay one of Jenny's eggs, as bright as silver. And there was a little path trodden and scratched by Jenny's feet, enclosing a circle just the size the blacksmith told him to make. He set to work at once, ate Jenny's egg, and then dug the trench.

Those three days were the happiest he had ever known. For he understood everything he did himself, and all that everything was doing round about him. He saw what the rushes were, and why the blossom came out at the side, and why it was russet-colored, and why the pitch was white and the skin green. And he said to himself, "If I were a rush now, that's just how I should make a point of growing."

And he knew how the heather felt with its cold roots, and its head of purple bells, and the wise-looking cotton-grass, which the old woman called her sheep, and the white beard of which she spun into thread. And he knew what she spun it for: namely, to weave it into lovely white cloth from which to make nightgowns for all the good people that were like to die. For one who wore one of these nightgowns never died, but was laid in a beautiful white bed, and the door was closed and no noise came near, and one lay there dreaming lovely, cool dreams till the world had turned round and was ready for that one to get up again and do something.

He knew everything! And he felt like he had never felt before! He felt the wind playing with every blade of grass in his charmed circle. He felt the rays of heat shooting up from the hot flue beneath the moss. He knew the moment when the vine was going to break from the earth, and he felt the juices gathering and flowing from the roots into the grapes. And all the time he seemed at home, tending the cow, or making his father's supper, or reading a fairy tale as he sat waiting for him to come home.

At length the evening of the third day arrived. Colin squeezed the rich red grapes into his bottle, corked it, shouldered his spade, and turned homewards, guided by a mountain peak which he knew in the distance. After walking all night in the moonlight, he came at length upon a place he recognized, and so down upon the brook, which he followed home.

He met his father going out with his sheep. Great was his delight to see Colin again, for he had been worried sick about him. Colin told him the whole story. And since back in those days marvels were much easier to believe than they are now, Colin's father did not laugh at him; he went away to the hills thinking it all through, trying to make marvelous sense out of what he had just heard. Colin went back to the cottage, where he found plenty to do, having been nine days gone. He laid the bottle carefully away with his Sunday clothes and set about doing everything just as usual.

But although the fairy brook was running merrily as ever through the cottage and Colin watched late every night, and even later when the moon shone, no fairy fleet came glimmering and dancing in along the stream. Autumn was there at length, and cold fogs began to rise in the cottage, and so Colin turned the brook into its old course, and filled up the breaches in the walls and the channel along the floor, closing all against the blasts of winter. But he had never known such a weary winter before. He could not help constantly thinking how cold and miserable the little, sassy girl must be, and how she must be saying to herself, "I wish that Colin hadn't been such a goon and lost me."

THE CONSEQUENCES

But at last the spring came, and after the spring the summer. And on the very first suitably warm day, Colin took his spade and pick-axe and redirected the brook once again. Down it rushed, singing and bounding into the cottage. Colin was even more delighted than he had been the first time, for this time he anticipated magical things. He watched late into the night, but there came neither moon nor fairy fleet. And more than a week passed this disappointing way.

At length, on the ninth night, Colin, who had just fallen asleep, opened his eyes with sudden wakefulness, and behold, the room was all in a glimmer with moonshine and fairy glitter. The boats were rocking on the water. The queen and her court had landed and were dancing merrily on the earthen floor! Colin lost no time.

"Queen! Queen!" he called, "I've got your bottle of Carasoyn."

The dance ceased in a moment, and the queen bounded upon the edge of his bed.

"I can't bear the look of your huge, glaring, ugly eyes," she said. "I must make less of you before we can talk, so you be heading less right now and immediately."

She waved her rush wand and laid it across his eyes. Instantly Colin saw that she and all of them were six times the size they were before:

"Okay—all good. Where is the Carasoyn? Give it me."

"It is in my box under the bed. If your majesty will stand out of the way, I will get it for you."

The queen jumped on the floor, and Colin, leaning from the bed, pulled out his little box, and got out the bottle.

"There it is your majesty," he said, showing the bottle to her but pulling it back when she tried to grab it.

"Hand it over," said the queen, holding out her hand.

"First give me my little girl," replied Colin.

"You dare bargain with me? Forget that! Hand it over!"

"Your majesty bargained with me first, and you know what the deal is. Give me the girl."

"Yeah, well plenty has happened since then. You tried to break our necks. You made a wicked waterfall out there on the other side of the garden which dashed all our boats to pieces. We were stranded on the shore and had to wait till our horses were fetched. Not pleasant! If I had been killed, you couldn't have held me to my bargain, and you ain't gonna hold me to it now. Give me the bottle."

"If you chose to go down my waterfall—" began Colin.

"Your waterfall!" cried the queen. "All the waters that run from Loch Lonely are mine, all the way to the sea. The waters are mine. But you messed with them. You went and ran my stream over a cliff by changing the course of the flow to direct it that way. Not nice! And all for your perverse enjoyment, I suppose. But it's no joke to me and mine. My boats were smashed to pieces! And you almost broke all our necks!"

"The water may be yours, but the farmyards are not, your majesty. And I can modify them any which way I please."

"I'll rout you out of the country," said the queen.

"Okay—go ahead. Do that. Meantime, I'll put the bottle back in the chest again," returned Colin.

The queen bit her lips with vexation.

"Come here, pretty child," she cried, in a flattering tone.

And the little girl came slowly up to her, and stood staring at Colin with a wary look in her eyes, as if she didn't trust his competence.

"Give me your hand, little girl," said he, holding out his.

She did so. It was cold as ice, but she gripped Colin's hand forcefully.

"Let go of her hand," said the queen.

"I won't," said Colin. "She's mine."

"Give me the bottle then," said the queen.

"Don't," warned the girl.

But it was too late. The queen had it.

"Keep your girl," she cried, with an ugly laugh.

"Yes, keep me! Don't let go," cried the child. Her cry ended in a hiss.

Colin felt something slimy wriggling in his grasp, and looking down, saw that instead of a little girl he was holding a great writhing worm. He almost flung it away, but recovering himself, he followed the girl's orders and grasped it tighter.

"If it's a snake, I'll choke it," he said. "If it's a girl, she's mine. I won't let go."

At that instant, the whatever it was changed to a little white rabbit. It looked him piteously in the face and pulled to get its little forefoot out of his hand. Although he tried not to hurt it, Colin would not let it go. Then the rabbit changed to a great black cat, with eyes that flashed green fire. She sputtered and spit and swelled her tail, but all to no purpose. Colin held fast. Then it was a wood pigeon, struggling and fluttering in terror to get its wing out of his hold. But Colin still held fast.

All this time the queen had been trying to get the cork out of the bottle. The moment the cork yielded, she gave a scream and dropped the bottle. The Carasoyn ran out, and a strange odor filled the cottage. The queen stood shivering and sobbing beside the bottle, and all her fairy court came about her and shivered and sobbed too, and their faces grew ancient and wrinkled. Then the queen, bending and tottering like an old woman, led the way to the boats, and her distorted courtiers followed her, limping and creeping. Colin stared in amazement. He saw them go aboard, then heard them sound like a far-off company of men and women crying bitterly.

And away they floated down the stream. The rowers dipped no oars, but bent and wept over them, letting the boats drift along the stream. They vanished from his sight, and the rush of the waterfall sounded on the night-wind louder than he had ever heard it before. But when he came to himself, when he got his bearings once again, he felt his hand had relaxed and noticed the bird—a lovely dove now—flying away. Once more there was nothing left to do but cry himself to sleep. What had he done wrong this time? He would do a thorough self-evaluation when the morning came.

Morning came swiftly. Colin rose from bed very wretched and headed outdoors to do chores. The moment he entered the cow-house, there, beside the cow, on the milking stool, sat a lovely little girl, wearing just one flimsy white garment and crying bitterly, "I am so cold. Do something."

He grabbed her hand, ran with her into the house, put her into the bed, then ran back to the cow for a bowl of warm milk. This she drank eagerly, laid her head down, and fell fast asleep.

Then Colin noticed something he had somehow overlooked about the girl. Although she had said she was about eight years old, her face looked scarcely older than that of a toddler.

When Colin's father came home, he was totally surprised to see the child in the bed. Colin told him what had happened, but his father was filled up to his tonsils with marvels. He knew there must be a more practical explanation for the sudden appearance of the girl. He told Colin about a troop of gypsies he had met on the hill that morning and that he guessed the girl was associated with them in some way.

"You were always a dreamer, Colin, even before you could speak. There's something to be said for that. I don't exactly mind. However—"

"But can't you still detect the lingering aroma of the Carasoyn?" asked Colin.

"I do smell something very pleasant, to be sure," returned his father; "but I think it's the wallflower on the top of the garden-wall. What a great blossom there is this year! I'm sure there's nothing sweeter in all Fairyland than that, Colin."

Colin couldn't disagree with that assessment. He decided to let his father's misconception slide.

The little girl slept for three whole days. And for three days more she never said anything other than "I am so cold!" But then she began to revive a little and to take notice of things about her. For three weeks she would taste nothing but milk from the cow, and would not move from the chimney-corner.

By degrees, however, she began to help Colin a little with his housework, and as she did so, her face gathered more and more expression. She made such progress that, by the end of three months, she could do everything as well as Colin himself, many things better, and everything with more order and style. So he gave up his duties to her, pretty much upon her demand, and went out with his father to learn the calling of a shepherd. Colin wondered whether she'd be pushing him out of that job someday, too! She had this controlling thing about her personality, and he never found it easy to push back. What's a guy to do?

Thus things went on for three years. And Fairy, as the two guys now called her, not only grew lovelier every day, but also began to respect Colin more than she once had, even though she knew he still had a lot of growing up to do.

Colin's father seemingly agreed. He sent him to an old friend of his, a schoolmaster, who promised he would stick enough education and maturity into the boy to make a big difference. But before Colin left for that adventure, he made Fairy promise never to go near the brook after sundown. He had turned it back into its original channel the very day she arrived. And he begged his father especially to look after her when the moon was high, for she grew very restless and strange at those times, looking as if she saw things other people could not.

When the end of three years education had come, the schoolmaster refused to let Colin go home. It turned out that, with good mentoring, Colin had become quite an exceptional student and also a reasonably cultivated young man. The schoolmaster insisted on sending him to college. And there Colin remained for three years more.

When he returned at the end of that time, he found his innocent crush on Fairy had swelled into red-hot passion. She was so beautiful and so wise that he fell dreadfully in love with her. As always, she was attractively bold and sassy, but now in refined ways that added a strange, hypnotic charm to her presence. Lovely she was indeed, and with such smarts and strengths, she was altogether impossible to ignore, fool or intimidate. She was irresistible!

And as dumb luck would have it for Colin, Fairy had been discovering—slowly but surely—that she was depressingly in love with him, too. But even better yet, albeit surprisingly, she had fallen for him just as he was and had always been. Plus now (but only as an added benefit) she was especially pleased how well he had turned out after having a mentor and college professors attend to his critical needs.

So all of this sealed it for both of them. They were deeply in love and wanted to spend their lives together. Colin's father agreed they should be married as soon as Colin bought a house that would keep Fairy safe, happy, and secure. So Colin went away to London and worked very hard till at last he managed to get a little cottage in Devonshire for them to live in. Then he went back to Scotland, married Fairy, and carried her off to make that new house a home. Married bliss lay straight ahead, Colin knew, aided by the peace of mind he would attain by taking Fairy far away from the neighborhood of a fairy queen who could not be trusted.

Part 2

THE BANISHED FAIRIES

Legend tells us that fairies had been doing wicked things for a long time. They played many ill-natured pranks upon adult human mortals, for sure, and had even terrified infants in their cradles. But they had also stolen children upon whom they had no claim and, when found out, refused to deliver them upon demand. To add to that, and as one final proof of their moral depravity, these no-good fairies routinely attempted to get rid of the obligations of their solemn word by all kinds of trickery and false logic.

It was not until the fairies had sunk this low in their depravity that their queen had begun to long for the Carasoyn. She, as if she were a human mortal, could not be ultimately happy while going on and on in a depraved way. Therefore, having heard of Carasoyn's marvelous virtues, and thinking it would stop her growing misery, she tried hard to get it. For a hundred years she had tried in vain. Not till gullible Colin came onto the scene did she finally succeed.

But not really did she. She had actually screwed up, and badly. She didn't know the Carasoyn made good magic only for really good creatures and just the opposite for really bad ones. Therefore, when the iron bottle which contained the Carasoyn was uncorked, its vapors suddenly changed her and all her attendants into old men and women fairies. They crowded away weeping and lamenting, weakened and wasted. And that was the last Colin had seen of them.

For when the wickedness of any fairy tribe reaches its climax, a punishment falls upon them. They are compelled to leave that part of the country where they and their ancestors lived for more years than they could ever count. They have no choice but to wander away, to be driven by an inward restlessness, still longing for the country they have left while barred from ever turning around and going back.

To compound their misery, they must always think tomorrow is the day they will go back home. But when tomorrow comes, they are always faced with another tomorrow. Until at last they find, not their old home, but the place of their doom, a place where their restlessness plants them, a place they can remain in only partial repose. Only partial, for they can never be satisfied with that place. They remain there only because their inward doom ceases to drive them further.

But this is not because the country to which they have been driven is ugly and inclement. It may or may not be such: it is simply because it is not their country. When a tribe is banished, it takes about forever before they can settle themselves into their new quarters. It's like their clothes do not fit them—they are constantly wriggling themselves into harmony with their new circumstances, never quite succeeding. It is their punishment—and it's a harsh one. Consequently, their temper is not always the evenest. Indeed, they are as much like human mortals as you might imagine, considering the differences between them. To sum it up, they get ornery when things are not going their way.

In the present case, you could say it was surely no great hardship to be banished from the shrubby hills, the bare rocks, the trickling brooks of Scotland, to end up in the rich valleys, the wooded shores, the great rivers, and the grand ocean of the south of Devon. That's what you might say. And you might say the fairies could not have been very wicked when this was all the punishment they got.

If you do say that, you must not have studied human mortals to any great purpose. Do you not believe that a man may be punished by being made very rich? What about the rich man who gorges himself on plenty and drops over dead at an early age with a heart attack leaving no will behind? And that's just one for-instance.

Anyhow, these fairies were not of your opinion about punishments, for they were deep-down depressed by this worst possible outcome for them. In the splendor of their Devon banishment, they sighed for their bare Scotland. For the big rivers and the leafy foliage of the Devonshire valleys, for the purple and green ocean that had seen ships of a thousand builds, and for the shoreline that was rich with shells and many-colored creatures—shores on which rested great old hulks scarred with battle and memories of Norsemen, shores that were a haven for whales and mermaids—they didn't give a tinker's damn. Rather, they longed for the clear, cold, open sides of the far-stretching shrubby sweeps, and the rocks and stones and the mountain ash and birch trees lining the solitary brooks of their homeland. The country they had left might be an ill-favored thing, but it was their own.

As equally odd as all this may be to you, and as surprising as anything a mortal might imagine, when banished fairies depart their homeland, their contributions to society are actually missed back home, and this is true despite the havoc and great sorrows they cause. For what happens to the livability of a country when the fairies depart is a kind of deadness falls over the landscape. The traveler feels the wind as before, but it does not seem to refresh him. The child sighs over her daisy chain because she cannot find a red-tipped one amongst all that she has gathered. The flowers have not half the honey in them. The wasps outnumber the bees. The horses come from the plow more tired at night, hanging their heads to their very hoofs as they plod homewards. The youth and the maiden, though perfectly happy when they meet, find the road to and from lover's leap unaccountably long and dreary. The hawthorn blossom is neither so white nor so red as it used to be. The day is neither so warm nor the night so friendly as before. In brief, that special something which no one can describe or be content without goes missing. Everything is commonplace. Everything falls short of one's expectations.

But oddly enough once more, it does not follow that the country to which the fairies are banished is so much richer and more beautiful for their presence. Not at all. For if that country has its own fairies, it doesn't need any more. And Devon, especially, has been rich in fairies from the time of the prophets and ever so long before that. But even supposing their landing spot had no native fairies around to quarrel with, it takes centuries before the new immigrants can fit themselves into their new home. And until they do, the queerest things are constantly happening.

THEIR REVENGE

But we have gotten slightly ahead of ourselves. This same tribe of immigrant fairies wandered through countless tomorrows before they finally arrived at Devonshire, their place of doom. And by the time they got there, Colin and his wife were already solidly settled down in their Devonshire farmhouse. But it did not take long for the fairies to discover just who it was who had come along before them.

An assembly was immediately called. Something must be done, but what to do was disputed. Most of them thought only of revenge upon the children. They were three—two girls and a boy— the girls six and four, and the boy two years old. But the queen hesitated. Perhaps her sufferings had done her good.

She suggested that, before coming to a final conclusion, they should wait and watch the household. In consequence of this resolution, they began to frequent the house constantly and sometimes in great numbers. But this waiting and watching kept stirring up their desire for revenge until the need to strike became unbearable. So the queen called another fairy assembly, and they unanimously decided to pounce.

But for a long time they could do the children no mischief. Whatever they tried turned out to the children's amusement. When they succeeded in enticing them beyond the home-boundaries, they would at one time be seized with an unaccountable panic, and turn and scurry home without knowing why. At another, a great butterfly or dragon fly or some other winged and lovely creature would dart past them and away towards the house, drawing them to scamper after it. Or the voice of their mother would be heard calling from the door, or something else again, but always something. Then at last, however, the opportunity did arrive.

One day the children were having such a game! The sisters had blindfolded their little brother and were carrying him now on their backs, now in their arms, all about the place. Now up stairs, talking about the rugged mountain paths they were climbing. Now down again, filling him with the fancy that they were descending into a narrow valley. Then they would set the tap of a rain-water barrel running and represent that they were traveling along the bank of a brook. Now they were threading the depths of a great forest, and when the low of a cow reached them from a nearby field, that would be the roaring of a lion or a tiger.

At length they reached the fancy of a lake into which a brook ran, and then it was necessary to take off the boy's shoes and socks so he could skim over the lake water on his bare feet. To emulate that scene, they dipped and dabbled around in the tubs by the water-butt that stood for farm and household purposes—now in this tub, now in that one.

The sisters, keeping their own imaginations alive, carried him through all the strange places inside and outside of the house. When they told him they were mascending a precipice, they were, in fact, climbing a rather difficult ladder up to the door of the hayloft. When they told him they were traversing a path-less desert, they were, in fact, in a vast, empty place, a wide floor, used sometimes as a granary, with the rafters of the roof coming down to it on both sides—a place abundantly potent in their own feelings to generate the sense of desert in his.

When they were wandering through a trackless forest, they were, in fact, winding about amongst the trees of a large orchard, which in the moonlight was vast enough for the fancy of any child. In the course of the story, and while they bore the bare-footed child through the orchard, telling him they saw the fairies gliding about everywhere through the trees. Not thinking that he would believe every word they told him, they set him down. For only a few moments they ran behind some trees to cause him additional amazement. That's when the child opened his eyes and saw the moon staring at him through the mossy branches of the apple trees, making it seem as if old, decrepit women, thin and bony, were all about him,. But his sisters were nowhere to be seen.

When the sisters returned after a few moments away, their little brother was gone. There was terrible lamentation in the household. But father and mother, who were experienced in such matters, knew that fairies must be in on it, and they cherished a hope that their son would yet be restored to them. Though often schemers with evil intentions, fairies also puttered in mischief that was sometimes brief in duration.

THE FAIRY FIDDLER

However, all their endeavors to find him were for nothing. Colin thought over many plans, but couldn't come upon the right one. Fairy dreamed up many too, but as bright and imaginative as she was, and as much as she knew about fairies, she could not devise one.

They were both so incredibly distraught over the loss of their boy that it was hard for them to think. They did not know they were dealing with the same tribe that had carried away Fairy when she was an infant. If they had known that, they might have figured something out right away.

After many months had passed, a night came when Colin was all alone; Fairy and his daughters were away on a trip. A few minutes after midnight, fast asleep and dreaming, he suddenly opened his eyes. He saw a few grotesque figures he thought he recognized dancing on the floor between him and the nearly extinguished fire.

One of them had a violin, but when Colin first saw him he was not playing. Another one was singing, keeping the dance in time. This was what he sang, evidently addressed to the fiddler, who stood in the center of the dance:

> "Peterkin, Peterkin, tall and thin,
> What have you done with his cheek and his chin?
> What have you done with his ear and his eye?
> Hearken, hearken, and hear him cry."

Here Peterkin put his fiddle to his neck and drew from it a piercing wail just like the cry of a child, at which the dancers danced more furiously. Then he went on playing the tune the other one had just sung, in accompaniment to his own reply:

> "Silversnout, Silversnout, short and stout,
> I have cut them off and plucked them out,
> And salted them down in the Kelpie's Pool,
> Because papa Colin is still a fool."

Then the fiddle cried like a child again, and they danced more wildly than ever.

Colin, filled with horror, although he did not half believe what they were saying, sat up in bed and stared at them with fierce eyes, waiting to hear what they would say next.

Silversnout now resumed his part:

> "Before the end of the month this year,
> Sweet babe will be left without eyes or ears."

Then Peterkin replied:

> "Sweet babe will be left without cheek or chin,
> Only a hole to put porridge in;
> Porridge and milk, and haggis, and cakes:
> Sweet babe will gorge till his stomach aches."

From this last verse, Colin knew that they must be Scotch fairies, and all at once he recollected their figures as belonging to the multitude he had once seen frolicking in his father's cottage. It was now Silversnout's turn again. He began:

> "But never more shall Colin see
> Sweet babe again upon his knee,
> With or without his cheek or chin,
> Except—"

Here Silversnout caught sight of Colin's face staring at him from the bed. And with a shriek of laughter they vanished, the tones of Peterkin's fiddle trailing after them through the darkness like the train of a shooting star.

THE OLD WOMAN AND HER HEN

Now Colin had got the better of these fairies once, not by his own skill, but by help that other powers had given him. What were those other powers? First the old woman on the heath. Indeed, he might attribute all of it to her. He decided he would go back to Scotland and look for her and find her.

But Colin knew the old woman was never found except by the seeker losing himself. It could not be done otherwise. She would cease to be the old woman—she would actually become her own hen—if ever the moment arrived when any one found her without losing himself or herself first. And unfortunately, since the time he found her long ago, but before he left for Devon, Colin had wandered so much over all the moor above his father's cottage that he didn't know how he could lose himself there any more.

But Fairy could! She could think on her feet like nobody's business and was brave in any situation. So she was well-suited for any adventure into the unknown. Yet the key for this adventure was not her formidable assets but rather her ignorance—she had not explored and learned the moor like he had and, smart as she was, she was directionally-challenged to boot! She could get lost in an open field under a clear sky! She was perfect for the task at hand!

But none of that mattered now! Fairy had left on a long shopping trip to the city with the girls to get an annual supply of food and goods for the farmstead. And the deadline for getting the boy back safe with all his parts intact would arrive before she returned. What a quandary!

But this problem of 'needing to be lost' needn't have troubled Colin. He had yet to learn there was a major exception to the rule. As it was, he simply needed to be lost somewhere. It didn't matter where he was when he got lost. It only mattered that he needed to be lost—wherever that might be.

Unaware of this, Colin decided he had no choice except to try to find the old lady and hen despite his knowing the moor above his father's cottage like the back of his hand. But sadly, Colin's purse was nearly empty—Fairy and the girls hadn't left him much money. They took almost all of it for their big shopping trip. So, seriously short on cash for the trip to Scotland, he set out to borrow money from a good and prosperous friend who lived on the other side of Dartmoor in southern Devon.

When he got there, he didn't find his friend at home. Now with even less cash than when he set off, but too short on time to wait to see if his friend would return, he set off back to northern Devon. He would try to tap another friend instead, a stingy one who lived nearby his home.

It was almost night when he started, and before he was many miles on his way, it got really dark. There was no moon, and it was so cloudy that he could not see the stars. He thought he knew the way quite well. But the track even in daylight was in certain places very indistinct, so it was no wonder he strayed from it and lost himself.

The same moment that he became aware of this, he saw a light off to the left. He turned towards it and found the light proceeded from a little hive-like hut, the door of which stood open. When he was within a yard or two of it, he heard a voice say: "Come in, Colin; I'm waiting for you."

Colin thought this was so bizarre, but he obeyed at once. Nothing much could surprise him anymore. He found the old woman seated with her spindle and distaff, just as he had seen her when he was a boy on the moor above his father's cottage.

"Jings! I wish Fairy was here to see this! How do you do, mother?" he said.

"I am always quite well. Never ask me that question."

"Well, I won't then anymore," returned Colin. "But cheese and crackers— I thought you lived in Scotland!"

"I don't live anywhere. I'm the real nowhere woman. But all who do as I tell them—exactly as I tell them—will always find me when they want me."

"How's your eyesight mother? Do you see yet?" It was almost strange that Colin should ask, for where her eyes should have been, there was nothing but wrinkles.

"Me see? You are still so slow, Colin. I always see so well that it is not worthwhile to burn eye-lights. So I let them go out. They are expensive, and I'm not doing so well financially"

"Yeah, me neither. Fairy is out shopping and I'm a little short on cash."

"I can't help you there. Anything else you want?" she replied.

"I want my boy. The fairies got him."

"I know that."

"And they say they have taken out his eyes."

"Yeah, well, I can make him see without them."

"And supposedly they've cut off his ears."

"He can hear without them."

"And they've salted down his cheek and his chin."

"Now, I don't believe that one," said the old woman.

"I heard them say so myself," returned Colin. "And besides, whether they did that or not, what about his eyes and his ears? Maybe you can make him see and hear without them, but no offense to you, that's not a good look!"

"How did he look before the fairies took him?"

"He looked a lot like me. A strong family resemblance."

"Well that's too bad. But let's get back to the cheeks and chin. Those fairies are worse liars than anyone I know. They always be blabbing out their fanny flaps. At the same time, something must be done. Sit down and I'll tell you a story."

"There's only nine days until the deed is done," said Colin, in a frightened tone.

"You think I don't know that," answered the old woman. "Therefore, I say, there is no time to be lost. Sit down and listen to my story. Here, Jenny."

The hen came pacing solemnly out from under the bed.

"Off to the sheep-shearing Jenny, and make haste, for I must spin faster than usual. There are but nine days left."

Jenny zoomed out the door, her head on level with her tail, as if a man with a hatchet had been after her. In a few moments she returned with a bunch of wool, as they called it, though it was only cotton from the cotton-grass that grew all about the cottage. The clump in her bill was nearly as big as herself.

Then she darted away for more. The old woman fastened it on her distaff, drew out a thread to her spindle, and then began to spin. And as she spun, she told her story ultra-fast. Jenny kept scampering out and in, and by the time Colin thought it must be midnight, the story was told, and seven of the nine days were over.

"Colin," said the old woman, "now that you know all about it, you must set off at once."

"I am ready, mother," answered Colin. Rising and smiling, he added a request:"But are you sure can't you spin me up a little cash?"

"No cash. Just keep on the road that Jenny will show you till you come to the cobbler's place. Tell him the old woman with the distaff requests him to give you a lump of his wax."

"A lump of wax. And what am I to do with it?"

"The cobbler always knows what his wax is for."

And with this answer the old woman turned her face towards the fire, for although it was summer, it was cold at night on the moor. Colin, moved by sudden curiosity, instead of walking out of the hut after Jenny as he ought to have done, crept round by the wall, and peeped in at the old woman's face. There, instead of wrinkled blindness, he saw a pair of flashing orbs of light, their shine reflecting on the fire rather than the fire reflecting in them. Then whoosh! The hut was gone. And the instant the hut and everything in it vanished, the cold fog of the moor blew upon him and he fell heavily to the earth.

THE GOBLIN COBBLER

When he came to himself he lay on the moor. He got up and gazed around. The moon was up, but there was no hut to be seen. He had disobeyed; he had not precisely followed the old woman's directions and was sorry now that he had been so foolish. He called, "Jenny, Jenny," but in vain. What was he to do? Tomorrow was day eight of their nine day lease. If he does not rescue his boy before twelve at night the following day, nothing could be done, at least not for seven more years, when their custom would allow him make a new appeal.

True, the ninth day was not quite out till about ten minutes past midnight the following evening, which by all rights should have got him another full day. But the fairies, instead of giving days of grace, no matter how justified, always take them. He could do nothing but begin to walk, simply because that gave him a bit more of a chance of finding the cobbler's place than if he sat still. But there was no way of knowing how to choose one direction or another.

He wandered the rest of that night and the next day. He could not go home before the hour when the cobbler could no longer help him. Such was his anxiety he neither ate nor drank a thing. But he failed to connect that as the cause of the gathering weakness that was slowing his physical processes down.

As it grew dark, however, he finally did become painfully aware of his hunger and weakness. He was just on the point of sitting down exhausted upon a great white stone that invited him to rest when he saw a faint glimmering in front of him. He was erect in a moment and making towards the place. As he drew near he became aware of a noise made up of many smaller noises, such as might have proceeded from some kind of factory.

Not till he was close to the place could he see that it was a long, low hut with one door and no windows. The light shone from the door, which stood wide open. He approached and peeped in. There sat a crew of cobblers, each on a stool with a candle stuck in a hole in the seat, each cobbling away.

They looked like little men, though not so little as fairy-size. The most remarkable thing about them was that at any given moment they were all doing precisely the same thing, just as if they had been a piece of machinery. When one drew the threads in stitching, they all did the same. If Colin saw one wax his thread, he saw that all were waxing their thread. If one took to hammering on his lap-stone, all fell to hammering away on their lap-stones with him. And when Colin came to look at them more closely, he saw that every one was blind in one eye and had a nose turned up like an awl. Every one of them identical in that way, though each looked different from the rest despite a very close resemblance in their features.

The moment the cobblers caught sight of him, they rose as one man, pointed their awls at him, and advanced towards him.

"Fine upper-leathers," said one and all, with a variety of harmonious grimaces.

"The top of his head—good bowl for paste," was the next general remark.

"Coarse hair—good thread," followed that. And so on they went, portioning out his body in the most irreverent fashion for the uses of their trade.

"Tendons—good fortified thread."

"Bones and blood—good paste for seven-league boots."

"Ears—good loops to pull boots on with."

Having come to his teeth, they said:"Teeth–decorative insets– after polishing." Then all gave a shriek like the whisk of waxed threads through leather, springing upon him with their awls drawn back like daggers.

There was no time to lose. Colin spoke out."The old woman with the spindle—"

"Don't know her," shrieked the cobblers as they advanced quickly with their awls.

"Creeps and crappers," cried Colin. "I-I-I-I mean...the old woman with the distaff!"

At that, all the cobblers scurried back to their seats and fell to hammering vigorously.

"Whew!" Colin struggled to compose himself. "I want you to know that she wanted me," said he, slowly resolving the quiver in his voice, "to ask the cobbler for a lump of his wax."

Every one of them caught up his lump of wrought rosin, and held it out to Colin. He took the one offered by the nearest and found that all their lumps were gone, after which they sat motionless and stared at him.

"But what am I to do with it?" asked Colin.

"He don't know what to do with it," broadcast the nearest one. "He don't have a clue!"

At that, the rest of the cobblers laughed, then called out in unison, "Forget him then. Let's use him for shoe material."

"Naw, we better not—the old woman with the hen is my grandmother," said the one nearest. "She sent him to us, and she's a worthy old soul. He's not the first dope she sent our way, and he probably won't be the last." And then, addressing Colin, "I will walk a little way with you and tell you all about it.

Colin stepped out at the door of the workshop and the cobbler followed him. Looking back to his rear, Colin saw all the stools in the shop suddenly vacant and the place as still as an old churchyard. And the cobbler, in his talk, gestures, and general demeanor, appeared a very respectable, conventional, little man. He proceeded to give Colin all the information he would need, and he also gifted him one of his favorite awls.

They walked a long way. Colin was amazed to find that his strength stood out so well, though his aching feet were causing him to limp. He had been walking many a long mile since he left his home and the soles of his shoes had worn thin.

At length the cobbler noticed and said, "I see, sir, that your shoes are almost worn to nothing. That's bad for your dugs. You really should take care of your dugs. They wouldn't bark so loudly and you wouldn't limp so badly if you did.

"My wife is supposed to buy me a new pair of shoes. She went on a shopping trip to the city before I left home to come here. It would have been nice to have had them before my long trip. But that's the way it goes."

"Would you like me to work you up a pair? They're great bits—only the best material. Quality material—that's our trademark. That's partially why I let you slide in there—no offense to you. But our bits are great. They cost, but they last."

"Yes, I would like a pair. But I've only got a few pounds."

"A few pounds? That's all you got? No way! We're tight and together here—no freebies and no discounts. And no credit! Straight cash laddie, or no deal."

The cobbler paused and looked to the sky. "I see the sun is at hand. I must return to my vocation. When the sun gets up, you will know where you are." He turned aside a few yards from the path and entered the open door of a cottage.

In a moment the place resounded with the soft hammering of three hundred and thirteen cobblers, each with his candle stuck in a hole in the stool on which he sat. While Colin stood gazing in wonderment, the rim of the sun crept up above the horizon. And there the cottage stood, white and sleeping, while the cobblers, their lights, their stools, and their tools had all vanished.

"I've got to write this down when I get back. But how can I make people believe it? Dad wouldn't believe it. Fairy would. She'd believe every bit of it on the spot. But who else? It does seem like fantasy!"

Even though the cobblers had vanished, there was still the
sound of the hammers ringing in Colin's head, where it
seemed to shape itself into words something like these:

"Dub-a-dub, dub-a-dub,
Cobbler's man
Hammer it, stitch it,
As fast as you can.
The week-day workman
Is wanting his boots;
The trip-a-trap fairy
Is going bare-foots.
Dream-daughter has worn out
Her heels and her toe-zees,
For want of cork slippers
To walk over posies.
Spark-eye, the smith,
May shoe the nightmare,
Bookies, footballers,
And the nine-footed bear:
We shoe the mermaids–
The tips of their tails–
Stitching the leather
Onto their scales.
There is but one creature
We never will do,
And that is the grifter,
No cash means no shoe."

A great deal of nonsense of this sort went through Colin's head before the sounds died away. And then, just like that, he found himself standing on a seashore, some distance, yet not too far, from his home.

THE WAX AND THE AWL

The setting sun was casting gold over the sea when Colin arrived on the shore. The tide was falling, and a good space of sand lay glittering in the setting sun. This sand lay between some rocks and the sea, and from the rocks, runners of water that had been left behind in their hollows were hurrying back to their mother. These occasionally spread into little shallow lakes, resting in hollows in the sand, but in a state of constant ripple from the flow of other little streams running through them. With the sun shining on these countless ripples, the sand at the bottom shone like brown silk, watered with gold lines flitting about like living things, never for a moment in one place.

Now Colin had no need of fairy ointment to anoint his eyes to make him able to see fairies. Most people need this, but Colin had developed a keen sense of fairy-sight over the years. He saw them in his nightmares and he saw them in reality—so to speak. His fairy-sight had come in handy, and would again.

As he drew near a certain high rock, which he knew very well, and from which many streams were flowing back into the sea, he saw that the little lakes about it were crowded with fairies, playing all kinds of pranks in the water.

Despite their wicked ways, nobody could deny it was a lovely sight to see them frolicking in the light of the setting sun in their gay dresses that sparkled with jewels (or what looked like jewels) flashing all colors as they moved about. But Colin did not have much time to be dazzled by the sight. They saw him watching, and the moment they did, they realized that this was the man whom they had wronged by stealing his child. So, startled by that, they fled at once up the high rock and vanished.

This was just what Colin wanted. He went all round and round the rock, assessing how to approach the job at hand. He made his way up the rock with difficulty; his shoe soles were so worn and his dugs were so sore. Then, without showing his face, he put his hand on the uppermost edge of it and began drawing a line with the cobbler's wax. He went creeping round the rock, still drawing the wax along the edge, till he had completed the circuit. Then he peeped over.

Now in the heart of this rock, which was nearly covered at high-water, there was a big basin known as the Kelpie's Pool. It was filled with seawater and the loveliest seaweed and many little sea animals. This place right here was the favorite resort of the fairies, and it was now crowded.

Colin continued to peek looks at the fairies and remained unobserved until they finally did see his big head come peeping up over the top of the rock. They immediately burst into a loud fit of laughter and began mocking him and making game of him in a hundred ways. Some made the ugliest faces they could, some queer gestures of contempt, others sung bits of songs, and so on. Meanwhile the queen sat by herself on a projecting piece of the rock, dangling her feet in the water, sulkily looking his way. Many fairies kept on plunging and swimming and diving and floating all the while they mocked him, a sight Colin would have enjoyed if they had not spoiled their own beauty and graceful motions by their grimaces and their gestures.

"I want my child," said Colin.

"Give him his child," cried one lustily.

Thereupon a dozen of them dived, soon surfacing with a huge sea-slug—a horrid creature, like a lump of blubber. They held it up to him, saying:"There he is; come down and fetch him."

Others offered him a blue lobster, others a spider-crab, others a clam, all while the rest of them sang mocking verses, each capping the line the other gave. At length they lifted a dreadful object from the bottom. It was like a baby with his face half eaten away by the fishes, only that he had a huge nose, like the big toe of a lobster. But Colin wasn't fooled; he had matured into a savvy individual. Granted, not so much as his wife, but no longer was he so easily taken in.

"Very well, good people, " he said, "I will try something else."

He crept down the rock again, took out the little cobbler's awl, and began boring a hole. It went through the rock as if it was butter, and as he drew the awl out of the rock, the water followed in a far-reaching spout. He bored another hole, and went on boring till there were three hundred and thirteen

spouts gushing pool water from the rock, and running away in a strong little stream towards the sea. He then sat down on a ledge at the foot of the rock and waited.

By and by he heard a clamor of little voices from the basin. They had realized the water level was getting very low. But when they discovered it was the bored holes that were causing it to escape, they cried with one voice of horror."He's got Dottlecob's awl He's got Dottlecob's awl"

When Colin heard this, he climbed the rock again to enjoy their confusion. He well-knew how fond these fairies were of water. Back in the day their main job had been to tend the flowers in which they made their homes, but also to do good works for every single thing that had any kind of life within it. That was their calling—for that special purpose they were created. Hence, at one time they were named 'Good People'. But after learning the great good that water did for the flowers and after sampling the refreshment it brought to them via the veins in the flower stalks, the fairies had fallen in love with the water, not only for the refreshment it gave them, but also the sheer pleasure.

Thinking only of themselves and not the good it gave the flowers that needed water to live, they began neglecting their business and took to sailing on the streams, plunging into every pool they could find. But they were far too fond of water. It had grown to be a total self-indulgence with them. And that especially included water containing salt!

On coming to the seacoast, they had found that the saltwater did much to restore the beauty they had lost by their exposure to the fumes of the Carasoyn. Consequently, they were constantly on the shore, bathing forever in the water. And especially the water left behind in Kelpie's Pool by the ebbing tide, which they found particularly to their taste. In fact, they had grown entirely dependent on seawater for comfort, so much so that they came to believe they were entirely dependent on it for their existence, or at least an existence they believed worth possessing.

Therefore, when they saw the big face of Colin peering once more over the ledge, they rushed at him in a rage, scrambling up the side of the rock like so many mad beetles. Colin drew back and let them come on. The moment the leader of the pack put his foot on the line that Colin had drawn around the rock, he slipped and tumbled backwards head over heels into the pool, shrieking:"He's got Dottlecob's wax!"

"He's got Dottlecob's wax!" screamed the next in line, he too falling backwards as did the leader, and this took place many times till remaining followers stopped approaching the line. Fact was, no fairies could keep their footing on the wax. And the line was so broad, for after Colin rubbed the wax on the rock, it had melted and spread so wide that not one fairy could spring over it, not even the most athletic. It was just as if they were in a prison.

The queen now rose to her feet.

"What do you want, Colin? Lay it on me." she said.

"You know what I want. My child. Cut the fake ignorance," answered Colin.

"Come and take him," returned the queen. She sat down again, not now with her feet in the water, for it was much too low for that.

But Colin knew better this time around. He sat down on the edge of the basin. Unfortunately, the tail of his coat crossed the line. In a moment half-a-dozen of the fairies were out of the circle. Colin rose instantly. There was not much harm done, for the multitude was still in prison. The water was nearly gone, beginning to leave the very roots of the long, seaweed tangles uncovered. At length the queen could bear it no longer.

"Look here, Colin," she said; "I wish you well. You know that. I've dealt fairly with you in the past, as I'm sure you remember quite well. If I hadn't, you never would have had a child."

She rose as she spoke and descended the side of the rock towards the water, which was now far below her. She had to be very cautious too; the stones were so slippery, though there was none of Dottlecob's wax there. About half-way below where the surface of the pool had been, she stopped, and pushed a stone aside. Colin saw what seemed the entrance to a cave inside the rock. The queen went in. In a few moments she came out wringing her hands.

"Oh dear! Oh dear! What shall I do?" she cried, "You horrid, thick people grow so much. This one has grown to such a size that I can't get him out. I just can't—he's too thick. I guess he'll have to stay. Sorry Colin. That's just the way it is."

"Will you let him go if I get him out?" asked Colin.

"I will, I will indeed. I suppose we shall be starved to death for want of seawater if I don't," she answered.

"Swear by the cobbler's awl and the cobbler's wax," said Colin.

"I don't swear by those, you fool" said the queen.

"By the cobbler's awl and the cobbler's wax," insisted Colin.

The queen reconsidered. "I swear'" she said.

"By the cobbler's awl and wax," Colin insisted again.

"I swear by the cobbler's awl and the cobbler's wax," returned the queen.

"In the name of your people?"

The queen squirmed as if she were a jellyfish in the sea. Squeezing out each word, she replied, "In the name of my people, none of us here present will ever annoy you or your family hereafter."

"Anybody missing, today?" questioned Colin, totally suspicious and cautious.

None of us here present or not presently in attendance will ever, ever, ever, annoy you or anyone in your family hereafter, thereafter, forever again."

"Just barely good enough. I'll come down," said Colin, and he jumped into the basin. With the cobbler's awl he soon cleared a big opening into the rock where his boy was imprisoned, for it bored and cut through the rock like it was butter. Then out crept his beautiful boy into his father's arms, his eyes, ears, chin, and cheeks all safe and sound.

Colin didn't hesitate to remove his boy and himself from the scene. He did not repair the holes he had drilled in the rock with the awl he had hitched to his belt (it would come in handy back at the farm). And he did not for one moment consider scraping and scrubbing away the wax—the fairies would have to take care of those chores themselves.

And though he paused to consider delivering a parting shot at the creatures who had caused him so much worry and trouble, he overcame the temptation. His mind was set on the peace, love, and comfort of home.

HOMEWARD BOUND

Colin carried his boy on his back; he was surprised how much he had grown over the past many months and was disappointed to find him acting so much a baby despite his physical development. But he knew immaturity corrects itself. Everything would fall nicely in place and back to normal soon after they got home. The important thing was to tote him there the best he could on his aching, blistered feet. Wouldn't Fairy and the girls be surprised and overjoyed to see the little guy when they got home? That thought, plus the outline of the adventure memoir he was forming in his mind, kept Colin going as he trudged along the road.

Their appearance on the porch near sunset was greeted with wild excitement and jubilation. Fairy and the girls smothered the boy with kisses and remarked over and over again how cute he looked. The celebration seemed as if it might never end. Once things settled down a little bit though, Colin tried telling them the story of his adventure and his sojourn among the fairies. But he stumbled through the story, and so often backtracked to correct himself, that he couldn't capture anyone's interest. Besides, the home-boy deserved and got every bit of their attention. And Colin perfectly understood this. He knew he would not have fared better with his story, not at a time like this, even if he had been able to tell it well.

As Fairy and the girls hugged and played with the boy, Colin took care of his feet. He was curious how the shopping trip had gone and anxious to take a look at his new shoes.

"Oh, I'm sorry, dear. I tried my best to find a pair that would fit your feet right and also fit your look. But I got lost searching for the store that everyone was recommending. So I had to give it up. You'll just have to find a cobbler nearby if you really do need a pair that bad."

"That figures. Perfect. Alright then—I'll find a pair somewheres. But tell me—you did bring some money home with you. Right? The money that you would've spent on the shoes if you had found a pair?"

"No. Sorry honey. I've got just a little bit left. I guess you'll have to wait until we sell enough grain or tatties."

"Sure. I guess I'll have to wait then," agreed Colin, as he looked down at his sore feet and shook his head in mild disbelief.

As days and weeks passed, Colin made some spare time to organize his adventure memoir with the hope that someday it might be published. He was reluctant, however, to associate his real name with the story because he didn't want to raise havoc with the fairies and bring their wrath down on his family.

His eldest daughter said a pseudonym would be a splendid idea. She also advocated substituting initials for a first name and suggested many combinations her dad should consider. Her favorites were JK, CS, HG, and JRR.

"I like the idea. And those are nice ones, too. I'll think about it. I really like the three-initial combination, JRR, because it's unusual. You never see that done, so it's perfect for the story I've got, which is way out there. But I like them all."

Soon, however, Fairy intervened and threw cold water on the whole idea of Colin spending time writing something that no publisher would ever accept. First off, it couldn't be a memoir because only people who have experienced fairies would ever accept it as fact, and there are but few people anywhere who ever have. And if Colin were to pretend it was all fiction, well, then it's a fairy tale, and those are for kids. No publisher would touch it because parents control the money pouch, and no half-attentive, up-to-speed parent would ever purchase a tale about mean and rotten fairies for their child to read.

Fairy concluded, saying plenty needed doing around the farm so there was no time for secondary pursuits that would lead nowhere. But even more important, they had a family to raise and they both needed to focus more time on that.

"And remember, you big, strong man," she added, winking and smiling, "we have to get and stay busy if we're going to have that baker's dozen we've talked about."

So Colin got and stayed busy with all the side-chores that came up on the farm. The barn needed painting right away, and plenty of other things needed fixing or maintaining—always. And as ever before, he did pay very close attention to his growing family and the woman he loved. He needed to be an excellent father and husband, and he was.

Still, he never could stop thinking about his excellent adventure with the fairies, and the old lady with the hen, and the blacksmith and his kids, and the cobbler and his crew, and the wonder and fulfillment he experienced rescuing Fairy and his son. And his constant thoughts about all these events and characters put them so firmly in his mind that he knew he would never forget them or have trouble keeping the details straight again.

Truth be told, as much as he loved his family, a part of him couldn't help but wish he could live these types of adventures again—his work on the farm was so routine and mundane. The best he could ever do though, he decided, was to wait until he could get some real, productive work out of his kids. That would free up some time for himself. And then he would put his adventure down on paper—just because.

Besides, times would change. Someday many people might believe in fairies, goblins, and demons. Or someday there'd be youngsters calm and steady enough to enjoy fairy tales filled with danger, and strange, magical adventures. He couldn't believe things like that wouldn't happen someday, which gave him hope for the future as he tended to his routine, mundane chores.

the end

THE CARASOYN

The Carasoyn was presented to readers in two stages. In 1859 Mac-Donald published *The Fairy Fleet* as a complete story ending with the marriage of Colin and Fairy. In 1864 he expanded it, renamed it, and published *The Carasoyn* as a final version. It's fair for us to speculate why he did this because there is no record or hearsay that explains what motivated MacDonald. The story has a mystical theme—that you must lose your self to find your true self. It's my guess that MacDonald wanted to reinforce this theme through repetition. Colin does lose himself a second time in the expanded version before he once again finds the old woman at the wheel, the higher power he needs in order to find himself. Colin relies upon her to complete both of his salvation missions, originally to save Fairy, then again to save his son in the expanded version.

Although MacDonald had success openly moralizing in his mainstay novels—readers were quite open to that in his day—he knew full well that words were useless in describing a mystical experience of God. As a person who practiced contemplation, he knew the best way to explain the experience would be to approach it indirectly. Symbolism is the name of the game when sliding meaning into a story indirectly, and MacDonald excelled at that aspect of creative writing. His series of fairy stories provided the perfect vehicle for him to practice his well-honed gift, and also to get his mystical message across to readers, or at least a fair proportion of them. Regardless, both for those who can interpret the symbolism and all other readers, his fairy stories, including *The Carasoyn* in both its early and final incarnations, are a delight to read.

Getting back to the matter of expansion, it's also fair to mention that, as the adapter of this fine story, I took the liberty of doing some expanding of my own. Most added material (including all narrative that follows Colin's trip home after he freed his son from captivity) naturally flows from my decision to enlarge Fairy's part in the story, which included recasting her as a more assertive character. And although I did not tamper with Colin's essential character, I did invent his dreams for the future, which also added to the expansion.

GEORGE MACDONALD
(1824-1905)

George McDonald was born and raised in a farming community in northeastern Scotland in 1824. He was a good student with a keen interest in the physical sciences. But soon after earning a Masters degree in both Chemistry and Physics, he underwent a spiritual transformation. He decided he would be a Christian preacher, and he gave that profession a fair try after his ordination in 1845. That didn't last long, however. He was quickly removed from his ministry because of his mystical orientation and unorthodox views on salvation. His congregation did not want to hear him preaching that everyone, including heathens and unrepentant sinners, would be saved.

Although his sermons cost him his pulpit, nothing would change his vocation. He remained a preacher until his death in 1905, but as an author of sermons, essays, novels and short stories. He made a good living as an author, primarily by way of his twenty-nine realistic novels. Though popular in his era, they were creatively unremarkable and ladened with heavy doses of straight-forward moral messaging. Consequently, his realistic novels are now almost entirely forgotten.

But not so his imaginative fiction! It remains highly relevant and popular to this day. MacDonald has made a lasting impact as author-moralist in both long and short fantasies for adults, adolescents, and children. He has even been labeled the grandfather of modern fantasy fiction. Many people, including noted fantasy writers C.S. Lewis and J.R.R Tolkien, believe that his fairy-tales are the best ever written. And remarkably, this holds true regardless of his intended audience. His gift for imaginative, symbolic fiction was so great that his tales generally transcend the ages of his readers. Whether written with adults, adolescents, or children in mind, most of his fairy-tales appeal to all.

MacDonald was the single greatest influence on C.S. Lewis (author of the *Chronicles of Narnia*), who wrote "I have never concealed the fact that I regarded him as my master; indeed, I fancy I have never written a book in which I did not quote from him."In addition, albeit indirectly, MacDonald has also gifted all readers, young and old, by way of his children. Lewis Carroll, intimate family friend, had them read his manuscript of *Alice in Wonderland*, then decided to publish it when they told him how much they loved it. Thank you, children!

Marc Johnson-Pencook is an illustrator, animator, and muralist. He lives in Minneapolis, Minnesota. His illustrations appear in books, periodicals, gallery shows and private collections, and his murals adorn many walls and ceilings in public places and private spaces in the Twin Cities and beyond. He also teaches illustration at the Atelier Studio Program of Fine Art in Minneapolis and the Art Academy in St. Paul. In addition, Marc composes and performs rock music—he currently plays percussion for Mod Gods of Nod—a psychedelic rock band based in Minneapolis. Marc can be contacted at: http://illustratormarc.com/

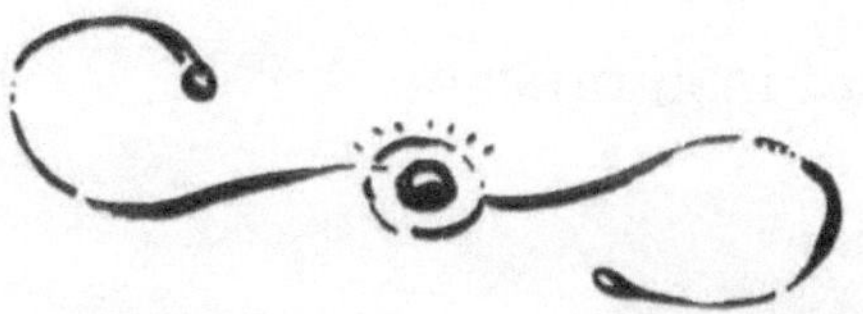

Jerome Tiller lives in Minneapolis, Minnesota. He is owner of ArtWrite Productions, a publishing company bent on making education and reading more pleasurable for youth. Adapted Classics, an imprint of ArtWrite Productions, uses fine-art illustrations to introduce classic stories to young readers. Learn more about Jerome and his company at: artwriteproductions.com and adaptedclassics.com